BUILDING BY DESIGN

ENGINEERING MOUNT RUSHMORE

BY KATE CONLEY

CONTENT CONSULTANT
Melodie Andrews, PhD
Department of History
Minnesota State University, Mankato

Cover image: Mount Rushmore sits among South Dakota's Black Hills.

Core Library
An Imprint of Abdo Publishing
abdopublishing.com

abdopublishing.com

Published by Abdo Publishing, a division of ABDO, PO Box 398166, Minneapolis, Minnesota 55439.

Printed in the United States of America, North Mankato, Minnesota
022017
092017

THIS BOOK CONTAINS RECYCLED MATERIALS

Cover Photo: Bucchi Francesco/Shutterstock Images
Interior Photos: Bucchi Francesco/Shutterstock Images, 1; Alex Pix/Shutterstock Images, 4–5; Rise Studios/National Park Service, 7, 32; Bettmann/Getty Images, 11, 37; George Rinhart/Corbis Historical/Getty Images, 14–15; Underwood Archives/Archive Photos/Getty Images, 17; Red Line Editorial, 20; National Park Service, 22–23, 25; FPG/Hulton Archive/Getty Images, 26; Shutterstock Images, 29 (left), 29 (right); Richard Clapp/Moment/Getty Images, 34–35; Charlie Riedel/AP Images, 40

Editor: Arnold Ringstad
Imprint Designer: Maggie Villaume
Series Design Direction: Laura Polzin

Publisher's Cataloging-in-Publication Data

Names: Conley, Kate, author.
Title: Engineering Mount Rushmore / by Kate Conley.
Description: Minneapolis, MN : Abdo Publishing, 2018. | Series: Building by design | Includes bibliographical references and index.
Identifiers: LCCN 2016962135 | ISBN 9781532111624 (lib. bdg.) | ISBN 9781680789478 (ebook)
Subjects: LCSH: Mount Rushmore National Memorial (S.D.)--Design and construction--Juvenile literature. | Structural engineering--Miscellanea--Juvenile literature. | Buildings, structures, etc.--Juvenile literature. | Buildings--Miscellanea--Juvenile literature.
Classification: DDC 624--dc23
LC record available at http://lccn.loc.gov/2016962135

CONTENTS

CHAPTER ONE

FINDING MOUNT RUSHMORE

Every summer evening at sundown, visitors gather in the hills of South Dakota at Mount Rushmore. People rise to sing the national anthem. Darkness falls on the great stone faces as the sun sets. Then a flash of light illuminates the mountain. The monument to great American presidents stands in a glowing light.

The ceremony at Mount Rushmore combines drama and patriotism. These are exactly the feelings that sculptor Gutzon Borglum had in mind when he first saw the

Sunset at Mount Rushmore can be a dramatic event.

mountain in 1925. South Dakota state historian Doane Robinson had invited him. Robinson wanted more tourists to visit the state. He thought sculpting a rock formation would attract visitors.

Borglum had experience carving mountains. He had recently designed a memorial at Georgia's Stone Mountain. The project has become controversial. It honors three figures from the Confederacy, the group of states that tried to break away from the United States in the 1860s to keep the practice of slavery. The memorial and Borglum were linked with the Ku Klux Klan (KKK), a racist and anti-Semitic group. Borglum himself held anti-Semitic views. Some historians believe he joined the KKK to get funding for the

PERSPECTIVES

SACRED LAND

Mount Rushmore is on land the Lakota Sioux consider sacred. The US government had promised them this land in the 1868 Treaty of Laramie. In 1874 miners discovered gold there. Three years later, the US government broke its promise. It reclaimed the land.

For millions of years before Borglum arrived in South Dakota, the rock formation that would later become Mount Rushmore had been shaped by nature.

Stone Mountain project. Others think he joined the group for political reasons.

Borglum was one of the world's only artists with large-scale stone carving experience. He accepted Robinson's invitation and traveled to South Dakota to investigate the area. The Native American Lakota people have lived in South Dakota's Black Hills for many generations. To them, this area is sacred.

ROBINSON'S IDEA

The land Borglum visited did not have any roads. Borglum and Robinson rode on horses to explore the mountains. As they rode, Borglum studied the rock formations carefully. How did sunlight strike them? Would the rock be strong enough to sculpt? Did large cracks ruin the clean surfaces?

When Mount Rushmore came into view, Borglum grew excited. The mountain faced southeast. That provided good light for most of the day. The rock was a fine, solid granite. It could be sculpted. It stood 500 feet (152 m) taller than the surrounding land. That would make a carving easy to see from far away.

Originally, Robinson had wanted the carvings to reflect the area's history. He imagined sculptures of Lakota Sioux chief Red Cloud. Nearby would be the explorers Meriwether Lewis and William Clark.

Their Shoshone guide, Sacagawea, would have a spot too. When Borglum saw Mount Rushmore, he had a different idea.

THE PROJECT MOVES FORWARD

Borglum began sketching his ideas for the sculpture. He wanted to honor presidents who had played important roles in US history. He chose George Washington, Thomas Jefferson, Abraham Lincoln, and Theodore Roosevelt. Borglum shared his ideas with Robinson. He agreed to the change of plans.

WHOM TO SCULPT?

Borglum chose George Washington for his skills as a leader in the American Revolutionary War (1775-1783) and for his work as the nation's first president. Thomas Jefferson wrote the Declaration of Independence and helped double the size of the nation. Abraham Lincoln had preserved the Union and ended slavery during the American Civil War (1861-1865). Theodore Roosevelt's leadership led to the building of the Panama Canal and helped bring the United States into the 1900s.

Robinson's project now had an artist, a site, and a subject. Robinson had also secured the needed permissions. South Dakota and the US government both granted permission for the carving.

With all the plans in place, Borglum organized a ceremony to dedicate the project. On October 1, 1925, more than 3,000 people attended the event. Robinson and Borglum spoke to the crowds.

After the speeches, bands played and soldiers fired a salute. At the mountain's top, actors dressed in historic costumes raised massive flags. The actors represented settlers from France, Spain, and England, as well as Native Americans. Each group had at one time claimed the mountain as part of its territory.

RAISING MONEY

Despite the excitement for the monument, the plans fell apart after the ceremony. The project did not have enough money to move forward. In fact, it did not even have enough money to begin.

Borglum traveled to Washington, DC, in 1926.

To get the project going, Borglum traveled across the country. He spoke to business leaders, journalists, and government officials. He wanted to find money and raise interest in the project.

Some money came in, but it was not enough for such a large project. President Calvin Coolidge vacationed at Custer State Park in the summer of 1927. The park was not far from the planned monument site. The president's presence drew attention to the project. It also brought in much-needed money.

That October, work on the sculpture finally began. Borglum would face enormous challenges bringing his vision to life. Along with a small army of workers, he would spend more than a decade trying to reshape a mountain into a monument.

It was on this sacred, stolen land that Borglum sculpted his monument. Many Lakota people were offended. They did not want the mountain defaced. They also disliked the men the sculpture honored. US presidents were responsible for thousands of Native American deaths. For some Lakota people, Mount Rushmore became a symbol of broken promises and heartbreak.

STRAIGHT TO THE SOURCE

Gutzon Borglum believed a mighty nation deserved a mighty monument. To Borglum, size was a reflection of greatness, as he wrote about in 1930:

> *Some few years ago, a sculptor visited me who showed me the head of a pin, on which he had carved the head of a president. . . . I began to think more seriously on the subject of making things larger and better. This pin-head sculptor was shaping the dimensions of his life and soul, whatever he had of either, into smaller and more cramped dimensions. . . . volume, great mass, has a greater emotional effect upon the observer than quality of form; that quality of form affects the mind; volume shocks the nerve or soul-centers and is emotional in its effect.*

Source: Gutzon Borglum. "The Political Importance and the Art Character of National Memorial at Mount Rushmore." *The Black Hills Engineer*. South Dakota School of Mines and Technology, vol. 18, no. 4, November 1930, p. 291.

What's the Big Idea?

Would Borglum's sculpture of the four presidents have been received differently if it had been smaller? How much of the appreciation of the sculpture has to do with the quality of the work, or the form? How much has to do with the size? How do quality and size work together?

CHAPTER
TWO

DESIGNING THE MONUMENT

With the site chosen, Borglum set to work. Carving a mountain was a large task. It could not begin without a design plan. He did this work at his studio in San Antonio, Texas.

The first step was to study the faces of the presidents he planned to carve. Borglum inspected paintings and photographs of the men. He looked at life masks and read descriptions of how the presidents looked. Soon he was ready to begin making a model.

Models allowed Borglum to test the design before committing to carving into the mountain.

The completed plaster model of Mount Rushmore stood five feet (1.5 m) tall. Borglum had made the model to a 1:12 scale. One inch (2.54 cm) on the model was equal to one foot (30.5 cm) on the mountain.

PREPARING THE SITE

Making a model was only the beginning. Next he had to prepare the site. The first challenge was transportation. Without good roads, Borglum could not get supplies or workers to the site easily. He asked South Dakota's governor for help. In July 1927, the state sent two crews to build new roads.

With the roads in place, a small city began to pop up at the base of Mount Rushmore. Workers could sleep in its bunkhouse. Borglum worked in its studio. Its blacksmith shop repaired carving tools.

The next challenge was making a path up the mountain. Engineers designed a staircase for the workers. It had 760 steps and several ramps. To transport tools and supplies, engineers built a tramway.

Before work could begin, roads had to be built out to the remote monument site.

It used pulleys and metal cables to carry a large bucket up and down the mountain.

Workers then set up a camp on top of the mountain. It had a repair shop for tools. Sheds stored supplies and sheltered workers when it rained. The powder house held dynamite. A small studio housed models. The top of the mountain also had several large winches. They raised and lowered workers along the face of the mountain.

PERSPECTIVES

MONEY VERSUS ART

The costs for Mount Rushmore grew over time. At some points, it seemed there would not be enough money to complete it. President Franklin D. Roosevelt, who took office in 1933, helped Borglum. He provided federal money for the work. In exchange, Roosevelt made Mount Rushmore part of the National Park Service. Roosevelt's secretary of the interior, Harold Ickes, hated the idea of carving mountains. He compared it to carving a person's initials into a tree. This outraged Borglum. He felt that his greatest work was being disrespected.

THE POINTING MACHINE

The workers needed measurements before they could start carving. Borglum made a pointing machine for this job. He would select a specific point on the model. Then he would give his workers the same point to drill on the mountain.

Borglum used two pointing machines. One was on the model. The other was on the mountain. Each pointing machine had a flat disk with the degrees of a circle marked on it. A shaft stood in the center of the disk. It had a long beam attached to it. The beam could rotate around the disk, similar to a propeller.

MEASURING A CIRCLE

Borglum's pointing machine was based on the degrees of a circle. A full circle has 360 degrees. A tool called a protractor is used to measure the degrees in a circle. Borglum's pointing machine on Mount Rushmore can be seen as a huge protractor. It allowed him to accurately transfer the measurements from his model to the mountain.

A cable ran out from the disk and hung off the beam. It could be lined up with the disk's degree markings, and it had its own markings for feet

BORGLUM'S POINTING MACHINE

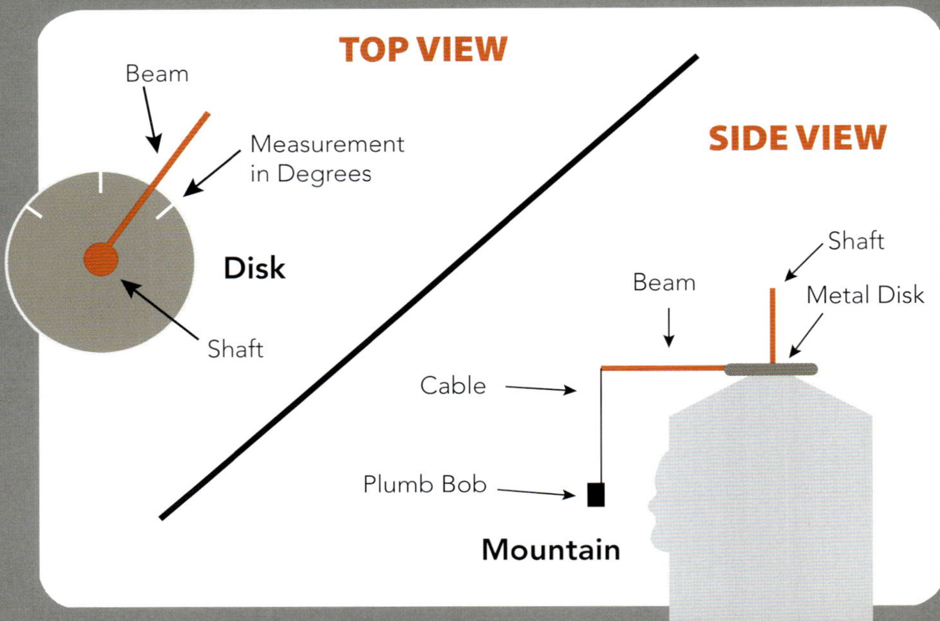

This diagram shows how Borglum's pointing machine worked. How did his system make it possible to transfer measurements from a model to a mountainside? Would this system still work today? Can you think of any other ways to transfer such measurements?

and inches. A plumb bob hung down from the steel cable, holding it tightly in place. This kept the measurements accurate.

Measurements could be taken in two ways using the pointing machine. A worker could measure how far, in degrees, the plumb bob fell from a central point on Washington's forehead. A worker could also measure how far a point was above the plumb bob by using the markings on the cable itself.

Borglum had stretched himself in new ways to create a system for carving a mountain. He had secured government money for the project. But it remained to be seen if his complicated plans would actually work.

FURTHER EVIDENCE

John Boland was a successful businessman from South Dakota. He was also one of Borglum's biggest obstacles to completing Mount Rushmore. The article on the website below talks about his role in the monument's history. As you know, every source is different. What new information did you find in the article? What evidence does the article provide of the challenges behind building the monument?

JOHN BOLAND

abdocorelibrary.com/engineering-mount-rushmore

CHAPTER
THREE

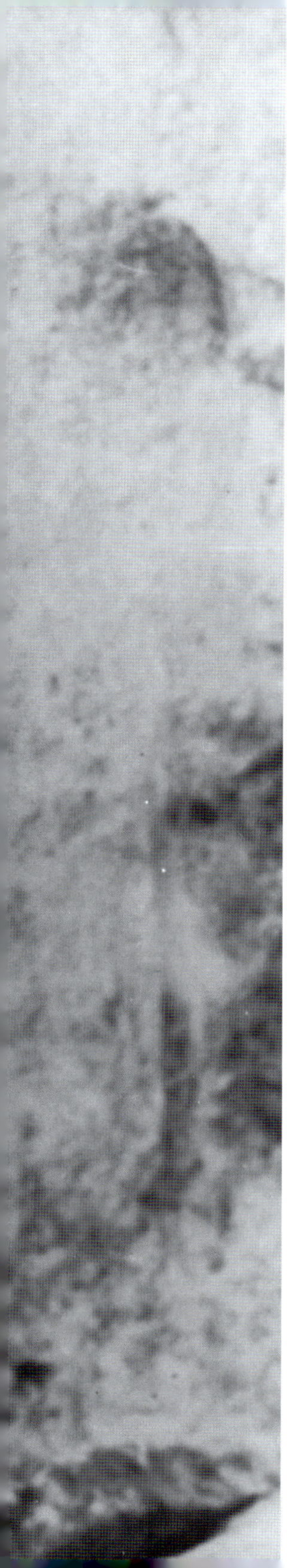

GETTING TO WORK

Despite all his planning, Borglum faced many unknowns. Geologists had warned him the mountain's granite likely had many flaws. They suspected it had deep fissures. They also believed the granite had blocks of schist in it. This soft mineral breaks easily. It could not be carved.

The only way for Borglum to know the rock's condition was to start carving it. He sent crews to the top of the mountain. They buckled themselves into chairs that looked like children's swings. Heavy cables connected each chair to a winch at the top of the mountain.

Borglum personally inspected the progress on the monument.

A winch operator then lowered the worker down the side of the mountain.

The first job was for the powder men. These workers set off dynamite to clear away the surface stone. This would expose the granite Borglum planned to carve. The powder men placed their dynamite in drilled holes in the rock. Then winch operators pulled them back up to safety before crews detonated the dynamite.

WINCHES

Winches played an important role in the construction of Mount Rushmore. A winch is a simple machine for lifting heavy objects. It is made of a large drum with a crank attached to it. One end of a cable is attached to the drum. The other end of the cable is attached to a heavy object. As the winch's crank is turned, the cable winds around the drum. This shortens the cable, lifting the object at the other end. The top of Mount Rushmore had six large, hand-cranked winches. Winch operators raised and lowered the men who carved the mountain.

A powder man prepares dynamite for placement on the mountain.

With the surface rock gone, Borglum saw white streaks running through the underlying stone. The streaks were pegmatite. It is a coarse-grained granite. Borglum was satisfied he could carve it. The project moved forward.

Slowly, the faces of the presidents began to emerge from the rock.

ROUGHING IN THE FACE

The first blasts formed the rough outline of George Washington's head. The next step was to locate the center line of Washington's head on the mountain. Borglum watched the light for several days to determine the best spot. With the center settled, the basic shape of the face could be carved.

Borglum used the pointing machine on his model to give workers their directions. Borglum measured each feature on the model. He gave the measurements to men called pointers. They located the point on the mountain that matched the point on the model.

Then they painted directions on the mountain for the powder men.

The powder men shaped the rock to the rough dimensions of the face. They used a jackhammer to drill holes in the mountain. Then they cut sticks of dynamite to particular lengths based on the pointers' directions. The skilled crews could blast away very specific amounts of stone. Twice a day, the powder men placed dynamite in the holes and detonated it. The monument began to take shape.

ADDING THE DETAILS

With the blasting on Washington's head complete, the crews were ready to add details. Drillers began working from the top of the face down. This way they always had a ledge to place a scaffold. The workers stood on the scaffold while drilling. The drillers removed stone to within six inches (15 cm) of the finished measurements. Drillers made closely spaced holes in the granite. This weakened the rock. Then it could be removed by hand.

When this work was done, the scaffold was removed. The next crew worked in wooden cages attached to the winches. They used bumpers on the surface of the face. These power tools vibrated against the stone gently. This removed the stone a fraction of an inch at a time. The bumpers smoothed and softened lines on Washington's face.

As the carvers finished their work, Borglum planned a dedication. On July 4, 1930, more than 2,500 visitors traveled to Mount Rushmore for the ceremony. Always interested in drama, Borglum did not disappoint. A massive American flag covered Washington's face. At a signal from the ground, winch operators on the mountain rolled up the flag and revealed the finished stone portrait of Washington.

SOLVING PROBLEMS

Borglum next turned his attention to the face of Thomas Jefferson. In Borglum's model, Jefferson sat to Washington's right. Starting in 1931, the crew

SIZE OF THE PRESIDENTS

This diagram shows the enormous scale of the carvings on Mount Rushmore. How does the monument compare in size to objects and structures you encounter in your daily life? What effect does its size have on how the monument is viewed?

followed the same steps they had used in working on Washington. They began by blasting away surface stone. Then they roughed in the hair, forehead, eyes, and nose.

Problems soon arose with the Jefferson carving. According to some sources, the rock was not suitable to carve. Other sources suggest that Borglum did not like how the two faces looked next to each other on the mountain. Regardless of the reason, all the work on Jefferson was blasted away. The crew started all over. This time they placed Jefferson to Washington's left.

This was not the last design change made to Borglum's model. As the powder men blasted surface rock away, more problems

PERSPECTIVES

DON'T CARVE IT!

Some people were not happy with Borglum's decision to carve Mount Rushmore. Some had environmental reasons for their opposition. One of these people, John Tjaden, wrote a poem sharing his feelings about it. The poem appeared in several South Dakota newspapers. The first stanza read:

> ***When God made our matchless playground, He did not intend that man should even in his wildest ravings dare come with hammer, chisel block and tackle, pick and mallet, to profane His age-old record, to profane the face of Rushmore by his puny, pygmy scratches.***

became clear. Areas where Borglum had planned to carve had fissures. He adjusted his model nine times. Each time, he had to check that the rock was good to carve. He also had to make sure the placement of the faces was pleasing to look at.

FINISHING THE JOB

Work on Mount Rushmore continued in starts and stops over the next several years. As funds ran out, Borglum had no choice but to stop work. Cold winter weather also stalled the work. As more money came in and the weather warmed up, he would rehire his crew and start work again. Slowly, they made progress.

As blasting and carving continued, Borglum's design began to emerge from the mountainside. By July 1939, all four figures had been dedicated. Detail work still needed to be done, but the monument was nearly finished.

The project received bad news in early 1941. On March 6, Borglum died following complications

Workers put the finishing touches on the monument in the last few years of the project.

from a surgery. His son, Lincoln, took over the project until it was completed that October. It had taken 14 years, but Borglum's mountain monument had finally become reality.

STRAIGHT TO THE SOURCE

Although no one died while blasting and carving Mount Rushmore, there were many close calls. One worker, Red Anderson, remembered a time when he and his winch operator miscommunicated, and Anderson had too much slack on his line:

> *I just flipped backward right out into space. I fell free for about twenty-five feet [7.6 m], then I hit the end of the slack. The jerk darn near snapped me in two! Then I slammed into the face of the cliff and just sort of bounced back and forth against it. Somehow I'd had sense enough to fold my arms in front of my face when I started falling. My hands and arms got skinned up pretty bad, but if I hadn't done that the Lord only knows what kind of a face I'd be wearing now. And I can tell you this: If you fall off a cliff and expect to be supported by a cable that isn't there it'll surprise you some.*

Source: Rex Alan Smith. *The Carving of Mount Rushmore.* New York: Abbeville Press, 1985. Print. 193–194.

Point of View

Do you think it is useful to think about workers' points of view when viewing monuments? Does thinking about these things increase the monument's impact?

CHAPTER FOUR

MOUNT RUSHMORE'S LEGACY

In the years since Borglum first traveled to Mount Rushmore on horseback, much has changed. It is no longer a quiet wilderness. It has become the bustling tourist spot Doane Robinson had imagined. Every year more than 3 million visitors travel to South Dakota to see Mount Rushmore.

The National Park Service (NPS) has made many improvements to the site. Tourists can learn about the monument at a visitor center. They can visit restaurants and gift shops.

Mount Rushmore has become the most popular tourist site in South Dakota.

UNFINISHED BUSINESS

Borglum's original plans have not all been completed. He wanted a large stone wall next to the presidents. It would be carved with important dates in US history. But the writing could not be made big enough for people to read it.

Borglum also planned for a Hall of Records behind the presidents' heads. He imagined it as a vault to store important documents from US history. It would hold statues of famous Americans and feature a huge bronze eagle over the door. Work began on it, but funding was cut so it was never finished. Today it contains information about the carving of Mount Rushmore. It is not a space visitors can enter. It is meant for people in the future who are interested in the mountain.

And they can explore the landscape on hiking trails. A heritage village honors the Lakota people who first lived on the land. Visitors can also tour Borglum's studio and see the equipment used to carve the mountain.

MAINTAINING THE MOUNTAIN

The NPS is responsible for caring for the mountain. Every year Mount Rushmore is exposed to wind, snow, rain, and heat. Over time, these elements

Maintenance workers over the years have hung suspended in front of the faces to inspect the ever-changing rock.

can cause damage. Park rangers are especially worried about how the weather affects the stone. If water settles in cracks and freezes, it expands. This can widen cracks and weaken the rock.

In 1989 the NPS began to study the cracks. Rangers mapped their locations. To do this, they divided a map

PERSPECTIVES

OVERSHADOWED BY RUSHMORE

Robin Borglum Carter, Borglum's granddaughter, feels Mount Rushmore unfairly overshadows his other artistic works:

> ***I think in some ways Mount Rushmore was the worst legacy that Gutzon Borglum could leave because he always will be known as the sculptor who did Mount Rushmore and yet at the time that he started the mountain, when he was 60 years old, he was well known for being a sculptor of beautiful monuments and beautiful pieces, and he was probably on his way to having a reputation as a great American sculptor. I think that was really overshadowed by Rushmore.***

of the monument into blocks. They identified four blocks that needed special attention. These blocks had major cracks. If the cracks in these blocks grew, they could shift other blocks in the mountain. This would change how the monument looks. The NPS study helped scientists understand the mountain's structure.

Rangers also examine the original sealant in the monument's

144 cracks. Borglum had used sealant made of linseed oil, white lead, and granite dust. Over time it had dried out. It no longer protected the cracks from water. Rangers removed the old sealant and replaced it with silicon caulk. This modern sealant can withstand the elements better.

In 1998 the NPS began to use a new system to care for the monument. It installed electronic motion sensors on the mountain. The system takes measurements four times a day. It is very sensitive. It can register movements as small as 0.0001 inches (0.00025 cm). Park rangers monitor the movements. Readings show that the carvings are stable and in no danger.

GETTING A BATH

Another effort to preserve the national monument took place in July 2005. That summer the NPS hired a crew to clean Mount Rushmore. It was the first time in the monument's history this had been attempted.

The July 2005 cleaning used high-pressure water to blast away stains on the monument.

Every day for three weeks, 15 cleaners climbed to the top of the mountain. They used harnesses to rappel down the faces. Using large hoses, the crew sprayed the faces with hot water. The cleaning removed dirt, dust, and grit that had built up over time.

Cleaners also removed lichen. These small plantlike organisms have roots that grow into rock. When the lichen dies, its roots leave a hole in the rock. The holes can fill with water, freeze, and expand. This can lead to cracks. Removing the lichen prevents such cracks from forming.

Cleaning and maintaining the mountain helps preserve it. Borglum designed the stone faces to stand for a very long time. He allowed an extra three inches (7.62 cm) of stone on all the surfaces of all the faces. Scientists estimate the rock will erode approximately one inch (2.54 cm) every 10,000 years. This means the work will not fully match Borglum's vision until 30,000 years from now.

EXPLORE ONLINE

Henry Standing Bear, a Lakota chief, asked one of Borglum's former sculptors to start a new project after World War II (1939-1945). He asked Korczak Ziolkowski to carve a monument to honor the native people who lived in the area. The result was the Crazy Horse Memorial, which is still being carved today. The article on the website below discusses this memorial. How does the planned memorial compare to Mount Rushmore? Why has it been criticized?

THE CRAZY HORSE MEMORIAL

abdocorelibrary.com/engineering-mount-rushmore

FAST FACTS

- The idea for carving a sculpture in South Dakota's rock formations came from state historian Doane Robinson.
- Sculptor Gutzon Borglum designed Mount Rushmore and oversaw its construction.
- Borglum chose to carve George Washington, Thomas Jefferson, Abraham Lincoln, and Theodore Roosevelt to represent the first 150 years of the nation.
- Work began on Mount Rushmore in 1927. The first face to be carved was George Washington.
- Borglum created models and new engineering techniques to carve the mountainside monument.
- It took 14 years to complete work on the sculpture. It was finished in 1941.
- Mount Rushmore is located on land that is considered sacred by the native people who live there.
- The US National Park Service oversees the care and preservation of Mount Rushmore.
- Every year more than 3 million people visit Mount Rushmore.
- Today electronic sensors monitor Mount Rushmore to alert rangers to any movement in the mountain.

STOP AND THINK

Surprise Me

When Borglum began work on Mount Rushmore, he was trying something that had never been done before. He had to invent many methods as he went along. What methods surprised you the most? How did Borglum's understanding of math and science inspire these methods?

Take a Stand

Over the years, some people have suggested adding more faces to Mount Rushmore. Are there other people you think should be added? What do you think of the original plans for including Native Americans and explorers? Write a blog entry with evidence to support your choice.

Why Do I Care?

Mount Rushmore has become a world-famous monument. Can you think of a time you have seen it in popular culture, such as on television or in movies? What effect did the monument's presence have on the movie or show?

You Are There

This book discusses the dramatic unveiling of President Washington's face on Mount Rushmore. Imagine you are at this event. Write a letter home telling your friends what you saw and felt. How does Borglum's dramatic and patriotic event affect you?

GLOSSARY

dedicate
to open or unveil something formally

fissure
a long, narrow crack

geologist
a scientist who studies what makes up Earth, especially rocks

life mask
a mask of a person's face made of wax or plaster

plumb bob
a metal weight that hangs at the end of a line to show a straight up-and-down line

powder men
workers who set off dynamite

rappel
to go down the face of a mountain along a rope

scaffold
an elevated, movable platform for workers to stand on

sealant
a material applied to a surface to protect it from water, heat, or other elements

winch
a simple machine that uses a drum, crank, and rope to lift heavy objects

LEARN MORE

Books

Coury, Tina Nichols. *Hanging Off Jefferson's Nose: Growing up on Mount Rushmore*. New York: Dial Books for Young Readers, 2012.

Kelley, True. *Where Is Mount Rushmore?* New York: Grosset & Dunlap, 2015.

McHugh, Erin. *National Parks: A Kid's Guide to America's Parks, Monuments and Landmarks*. New York: Black Dog & Leventhal Publishers, 2012.

Websites

To learn more about Building by Design, visit **abdobooklinks.com**. These links are routinely monitored and updated to provide the most current information available.

Visit **abdocorelibrary.com** for free additional tools for teachers and students.

INDEX

About the Author

Kate Conley has been writing nonfiction books for children for nearly two decades. When she's not writing, Conley spends her time reading, sewing, and solving crossword puzzles. She lives in Minnesota with her husband and two children.